ready, steady, r

The Little Pink Book
of the Woolly Mammoth

Angie Sage

Puffin Books

PUFFIN BOOKS

Published by the Penguin Group
Penguin Books Ltd, 27 Wrights Lane, London W8 5TZ, England
Penguin Books USA Inc., 375 Hudson Street, New York, New York 10014, USA
Penguin Books Australia Ltd, Ringwood, Victoria, Australia
Penguin Books Canada Ltd, 10 Alcorn Avenue, Toronto, Ontario, Canada M4V 3B2
Penguin Books (NZ) Ltd, 182–190 Wairau Road, Auckland 10, New Zealand

Penguin Books Ltd, Registered Offices: Harmondsworth, Middlesex, England

Published in Puffin Books 1994
10 9 8 7 6 5 4 3 2 1

The moral right of the author/illustrator has been asserted

Filmset in Monotype Bembo Schoolbook

Reproduction by Anglia Graphics Ltd, Bedford

Made and printed in Great Britain by William Clowes Ltd, Beccles and London

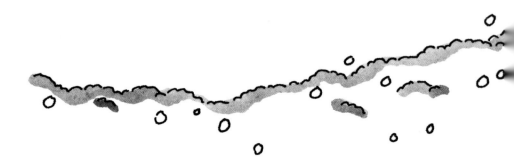

Introducing one woolly mammoth
in a snowstorm.

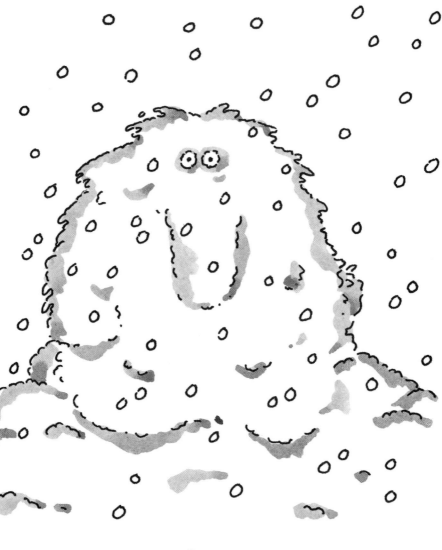

Introducing lots of woolly
mammoths in a snowstorm.

They are:

Gran
Mammoth

Mum
Mammoth

Dad
Mammoth

friends...

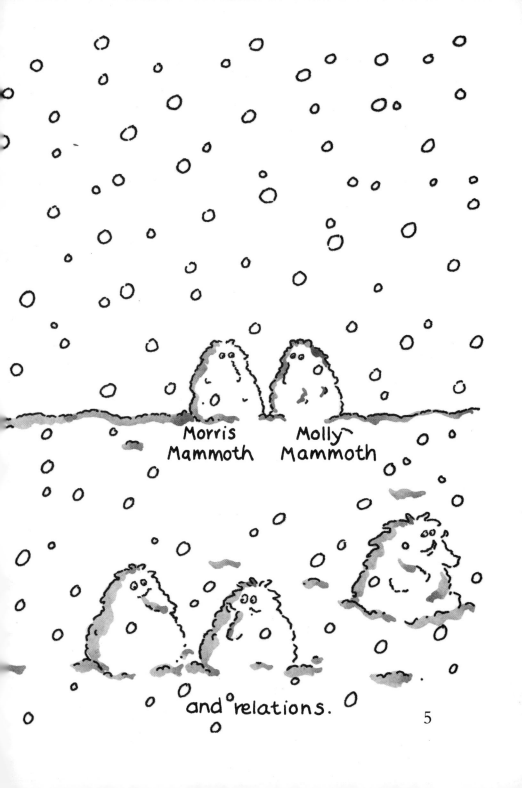

Morris
Mammoth

Molly
Mammoth

and relations.

5

Gran, Mum, Dad, Morris and
Molly Mammoth lived above
Gran's Mammoth Woolly Shop.

They lived underneath the glacier
at the end of Glacier Street.
(A glacier is a giant frozen river.)

They liked living there because it
was always cold. Mammoths did
not like hot weather.

Gran Mammoth knitted mammoth woollies. Woolly jumpers, woolly socks, woolly hats, woolly mitts, woolly vests and woolly knickers – woolly anything, in fact.

Even Fang, Gran's sabre-toothed cat, wore a woolly catsuit.

9

All the mammoths in the town
wore Gran's woollies. This was
partly because it never stopped
snowing and partly because they
liked wearing woollies.

11

But one day in the middle of
summer it stopped snowing.

The sun came out.

"What's that, Gran?" asked Molly.

"I've heard about that," said
Gran, "and no good will come
of it, mark my words."

And no good did come of it. Well,
not for a while, anyway.

The glacier started dripping.

There were puddles on the floor,
puddles in the bath and puddles
in the beds.

Molly was upset.

Gran opened all the fridge doors,
but still the glacier dripped and
splashed and sploshed.

Drip . . . splash . . . splosh.

Morris and Molly went paddling.

17

One evening Mum Mammoth and
Dad Mammoth came home from
work early.

Mum took off her woolly scarf
and hat.

21

A few days later there was a
mammoth queue leading to . . .

23

. . . Gran's Mammoth Woolly shop.

There was a sign in the window. It said:

Gran was not pleased.

But wait — who's this?

"Who's there?"

"The woolly penguin who?"

"It's the woolly penguin," said
Molly.

The woolly penguin had a
flipperful of tickets.

Here are your tickets
for the last ice-floe
to the Frozen North

And so Molly, Morris, Dad, Mum
and Gran Mammoth caught the
last ice-floe to the Frozen North.

So did 562 other mammoths.
That was every single mammoth
in the town.

Now, here is a question:

"How do you get 567 mammoths
(and one sabre-toothed cat) on an
ice-floe?"

Answer:

"You ask them all to breathe in
and stand on tiptoe."

33

Here is another question:
"What do you do when the sun
keeps shining, you cannot find the
Frozen North, and the ice-floe
starts to melt?"

This is what one woolly penguin
wanted to know.

This is what 567 mammoths
wanted to know too. The ice-floe
floated in the sunshine and got
smaller . . . and smaller . . . and
smaller.

The pile of mammoths got higher
. . . and higher . . . and higher.

38

Molly was on the top. Molly could see something. Molly thought it was the Frozen North.

"I can see it, I can see it!" shouted Molly. "I can see the Frozen North!"

"Hurry, hurry!" said the woolly penguin, who was very worried that someone would step on him and not notice.

So they blew . . .

. . . and they blew, right into the mouth of a huge blue whale.

Suddenly it went dark.

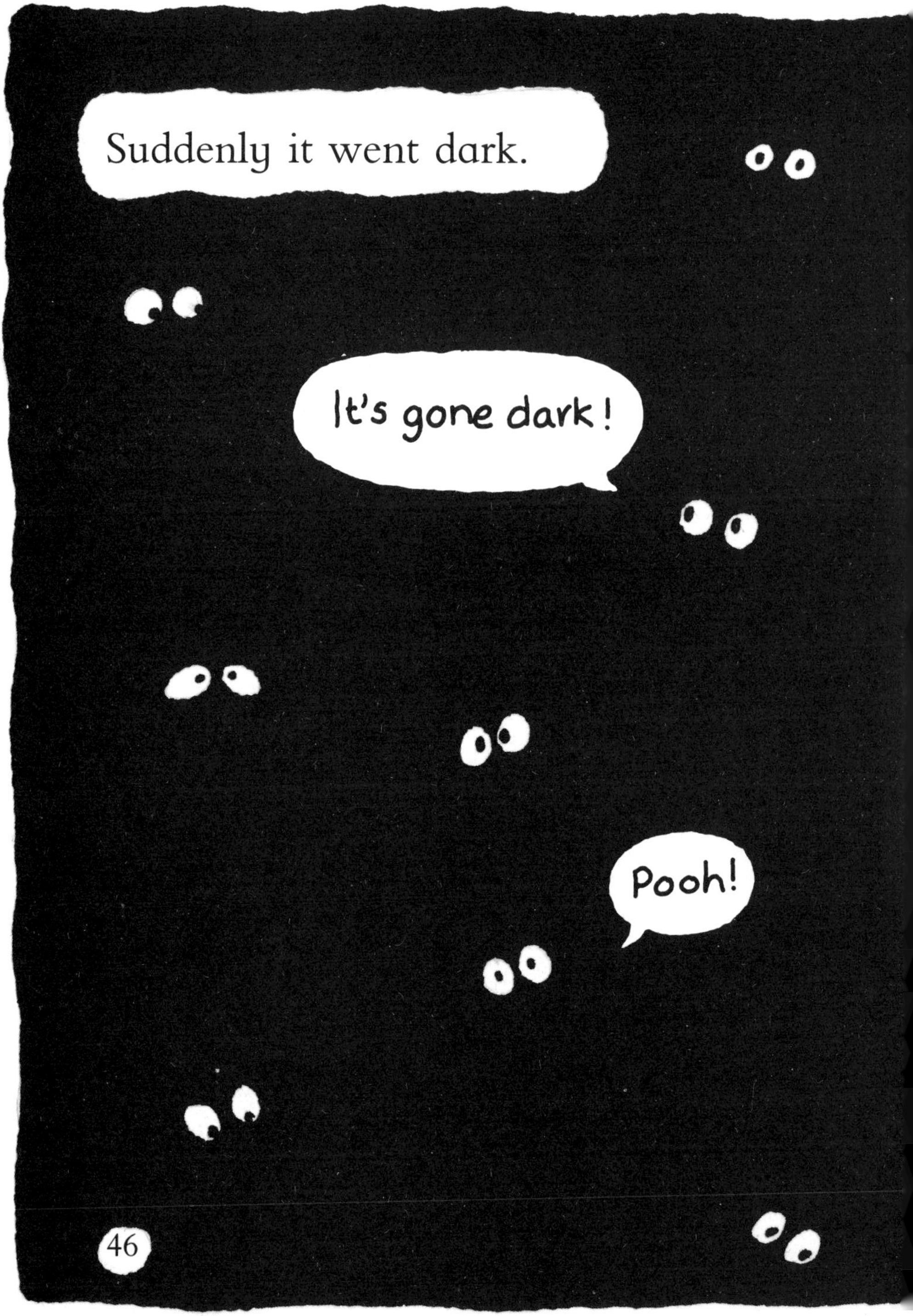

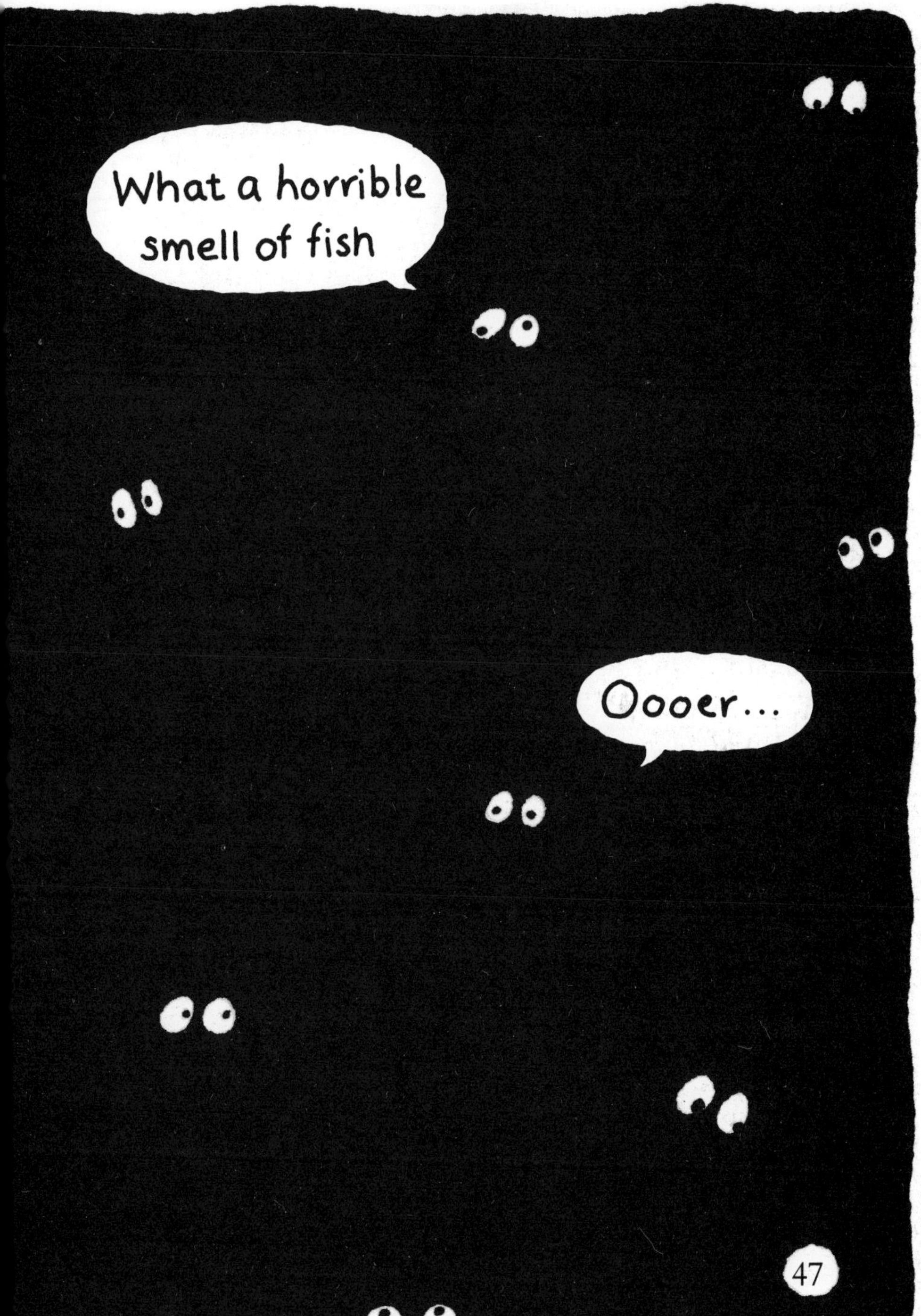
What a horrible smell of fish
Oooer...

Just then, a certain whale realized
that she did not feel very well.

She dived down . . .

51

. . . down, down, down through
the deep, dark, cold sea.

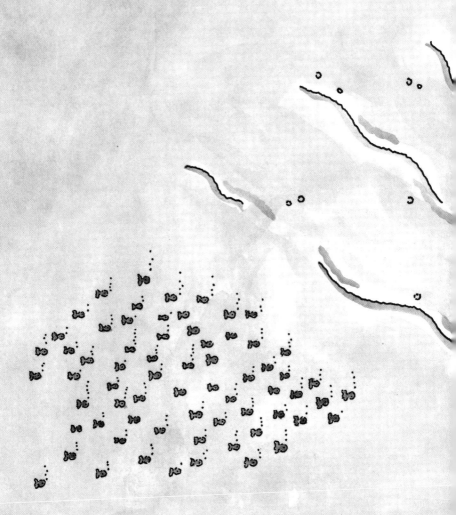

53

Then she came up, up, up into the snowy lands of the Frozen North.

She left a lot of wet, fishy
mammoths, one wet, fishy sabre-
toothed cat and a very happy
woolly penguin standing in a
snowstorm.

"It's snowing, Gran," said Molly,
"and that sun thing has gone!"
Gran got out her knitting.

Mum and Dad took off their sun-
glasses and went to build a house.
Morris made a snow mammoth.

And Molly?

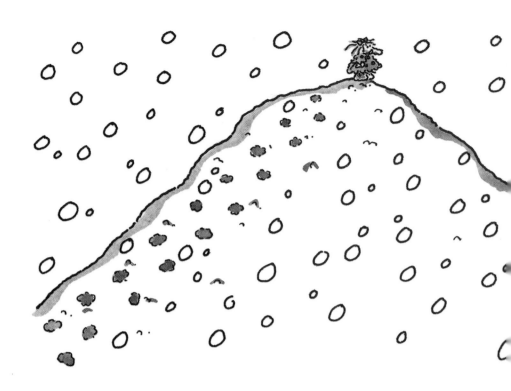

Molly climbed to the top of the
nearest hill. All around she could
see nothing but snow.

"This really *is* the Frozen North,"
she thought. "I wonder where we
are?"

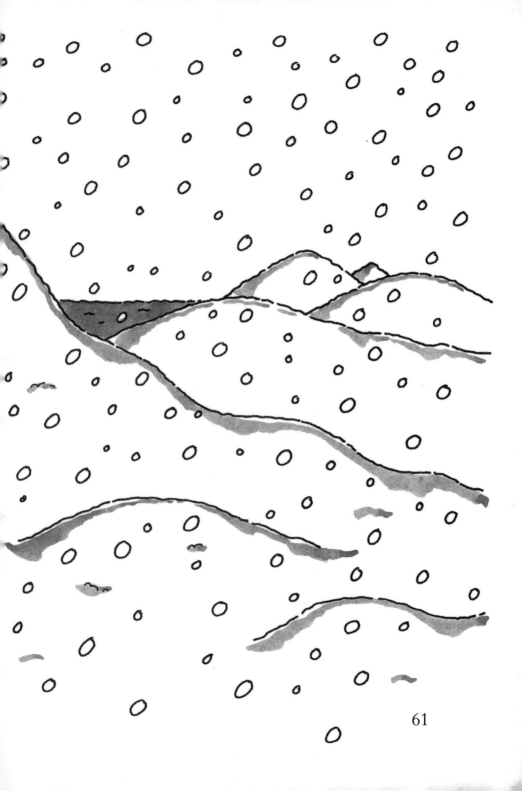

61

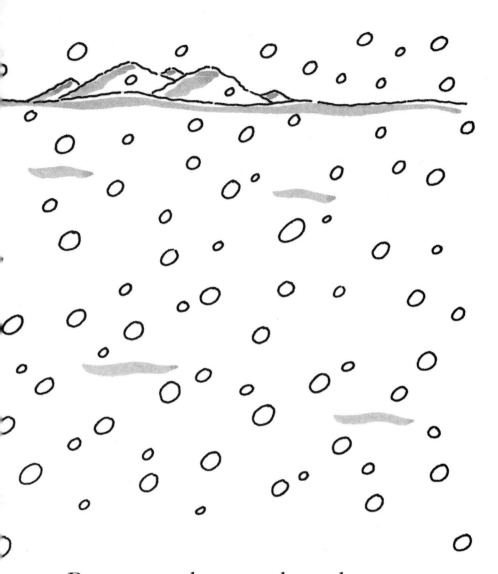

But no one knows where the
mammoths are, because no one
has found them . . . yet.

ready, steady, read!

Other books in this series